Herbster Readers

JUMPING INTO THE POOL

Written by Joanne Meier and Cecilia Minden • Illustrated by Bob Ostrom
Created by Herbie J. Thorpe

ABOUT THE AUTHORS

Joanne Meier, PhD, has worked as an elementary school teacher, university professor, and researcher. She earned her BA in early childhood education from the University of South Carolina, and her MEd and PhD in education from the University of Virginia. She currently works as a literacy consultant for schools and private organizations. Joanne lives in Virginia with her husband Eric, daughters Kella and Erin, two cats, and a gerbil.

Cecilia Minden, PhD, is the former director of the Language and Literacy Program at the Harvard Graduate School of Education. She is now a reading consultant for school and library publications. She earned her PhD in reading education from the University of Virginia. Cecilia and her husband, Dave Cupp, live outside Chapel Hill, North Carolina. They enjoy sharing their love of reading with their grandchildren, Chelsea and Qadir.

ABOUT THE ILLUSTRATOR

Bob Ostrom has been illustrating children's books for nearly twenty years. A graduate of the New England School of Art & Design at Suffolk University, Bob has worked for such companies as Disney, Nickelodeon, and Cartoon Network. He lives in North Carolina with his wife Melissa and three children, Will, Charlie, and Mae.

ABOUT THE SERIES CREATOR

Herbie J. Thorpe had long envisioned a beginning-readers' series about a fun, energetic bear with a big imagination. Herbie is a book lover and an avid supporter of libraries and the role they play in fostering the love of reading. He consults with librarians and matches them with the perfect books for their students and patrons. He lives in Louisiana with his wife Misty and their daughter Carson.

The Child's World®

Published in the United States of America by The Child's World®
1980 Lookout Drive • Mankato, MN 56003-1705
800-599-READ • www.childsworld.com

Acknowledgments
The Child's World®: Mary Berendes, Publishing Director
The Design Lab: Kathleen Petelinsek, Design;
Gregory Lindholm, Page Production
Assistant colorist: Richard Carbajal

Library of Congress Cataloging-in-Publication Data
Meier, Joanne D.
  Jumping into the pool / by Joanne Meier and Cecilia Minden ;
illustrated by Bob Ostrom.
    p. cm. — (Herbster readers)
  Summary: "In this simple story belonging to the third level of
Herbster Readers, young Herbie is scared to go underwater
but is helped by his imagination."—Provided by publisher.
  ISBN 978-1-60253-017-1 (library bound : alk. paper)
  [1. Swimming—Fiction. 2. Bears—Fiction.] I. Minden, Cecilia.
II. Ostrom, Bob, ill. III. Title.
  PZ7.M5148Jum 2008
  [E]—dc22   2008002596

Herbie Bear's family was at the pool.

"Come on, Herbie! Jump in!"
shouted Hannah.

Herbie stood at the edge of the pool.

He watched his sister swim.

"I'll just use the stairs," said Herbie.

7

He walked across the pool deck.

Herbie felt embarrassed.

He walked toward the stairs
in the shallow end.

Samantha's kindergarten friends were playing on the stairs.

Herbie felt too old to be
in this end of the pool!

Herbie wanted to go under.
He wanted to learn to swim.

He just couldn't do it!

He was scared to go under.

TWEEEEET!

The lifeguard blew her whistle.

TWEEEEET!

"All kids out of the pool.
Time for adult swim."

The kids climbed out. They found
chairs in the hot sun.

Herbie sat and stared into the water.

"Help!" cried Hannah. "My favorite necklace sank to the bottom!"

"I'll get it!" shouted Herbie.

Herbie jumped in and swam to the bottom.

He grabbed Hannah's necklace.

"Thanks!" said Hannah.
"You're a great swimmer!"

"It's easy," said Herbie.

"Just hold your breath and kick your legs!
Bears are great swimmers."

TWEEEEET!

The lifeguard blew her whistle.
Break time was over.

Everyone jumped back into the pool.

"Come on, Herbie! Jump in!"
shouted Hannah.

Herbie Bear just smiled—and jumped in.